COMIC CHAPTER BOOKS

DC COMICS™
SUPER HEROES

SUPERMAN

STONE ARCH BOOKS
a capstone imprint

Superman: Comic Chapter Books are published by
Stone Arch Books,
A Capstone Imprint
1710 Roe Crest Drive
North Mankato, Minnesota 56003
www.capstoneyoungreaders.com

Star33542

Library of Congress Cataloging-in-Publication Data is available on the Library of Congress website.

ISBN: 978-1-4342-9134-9 (library binding)

ISBN: 978-1-4342-9138-7 (paperback

ISBN: 978-1-4965-0096-0 (eBook)

Summary: Lex Luthor is up to his old tricks again. Wearing his battle suit, the super-villain sets out to steal a special chip from S.T.A.R Labs, called the Mega Module with the help of a few friends. Superman shows up just in time to stop Lex's pals, but Lex manages to insert the Mega Module into his suit before Superman can stop him. Now, with power levels similar to Superman's, Lex is looking to steal Superman's claim to fame as the real Man of Steel!

Printed in the United States of America in Stevens Point, Wisconsin.
032014 008092WZF14

COMIC CHAPTER BOOKS

DC COMICS™ SUPER HEROES

SUPERMAN

THE REAL MAN OF STEEL

written by
Laurie S. Sutton

illustrated by
Luciano Vecchio

TABLE OF CONTENTS

CHAPTER 1

BOOM!

The solid steel security doors to the "Top Secret" levels of S.T.A.R. Labs crashed open. A giant, muscular being stepped through the entrance. He watched the technicians run away in fear.

"You'd better run, you little ants!" Solomon Grundy said with satisfaction.

"Stop blocking the door," said a woman as tall as he was. She pushed him forward.

Solomon Grundy grunted. "Hey! Quit shoving, Giganta!" the greedy zombie complained.

"Stand aside, both of you," said a thin man in a blue wizard's outfit. "You two may look like brutes, but you don't have to act like it." He pushed past them and strode through the smashed doorway like a lord entering a mansion.

Solomon Grundy grabbed the heavy metal door and angrily threw it across the room. "Grrrrahhhhh!"

CRAAAASH!

It made a hole in the wall as big as a truck. Lab workers on the other side of the wall cried out in surprise. When they saw Solomon Grundy and Giganta, they ran.

"Your methods are crude, but effective," the wizard said. He walked calmly toward the new opening.

As the wizard entered the lab, he began to conjure a seeking spell.

ZWOOSH!

A globe of magic floated around the room as if examining it.

FZZZZZT!

The globe dissolved in a fizzle of light. "The module isn't in here," the wizard said. "We need to keep searching."

"Ha! My turn!" Giganta laughed. She used her enormous heel to kick in the next steel door.

KER-SMASH!

They entered a large chamber. Workers scrambled to hide under desks and behind equipment.

But before the trio of super-villains could move forward, they were attacked from behind.

ZAP!

ZAP!

ZAP!

Energy blasts from powerful stun weapons opened fire all around them.

"Freeze!" a voice commanded. "Those were just warning shots."

The wizard, Giganta, and Solomon Grundy turned around. They saw a squad of S.T.A.R. Labs security guards. The trio of villains tilted their heads in confusion.

"Surrender quietly and no one gets hurt," said the officer in charge.

The super-villains looked at each other. Then they laughed.

"We don't know how to be quiet," Giganta informed the officer.

"SMASH" AND "CRASH" ARE TWO OF MY FAVORITE WORDS!
SMASH!!
CRASHH!!
ZZZTT!
HA! THAT TICKLES.
ZZZTT!
ZZZTT!
ZZZTT!
SUDDENLY...
ZZZTT!
ZZZTT!
ZZZTT!
OBVIOUSLY, IF I WANT SOMETHING DONE RIGHT, I HAVE TO DO IT MYSELF.

Lex Luthor walked calmly into the wrecked lab. He wore his armored battle suit. It was the reason that he and the others were breaking into S.T.A.R. Labs.

"Have you found the Mega Module yet?" Luthor asked. "It will give my battle suit the power to finally defeat Superman."

"Not yet," the wizard replied.

"Why not?" Luthor growled. "Your magic is why I assigned you to this mission."

The wizard grunted, then he conjured another seeking spell. This time the glowing globe raced away, passing through a wall.

SWOOOOSH!

"My spell is working!" the wizard said. "What you seek is on the other side of this wall." The wizard pointed at the steel wall in front of them.

Solomon Grundy didn't hesitate.

CRRRRRASSSSH!

He smashed through the metal wall. Giganta grabbed the torn edges.

SCREEEEEECH!

She pulled them back like they were aluminum foil. Luthor stepped through the opening. An object the size and shape of an ostrich egg sat on a display stand in the middle of the chamber.

"Ah, the Mega Module," Luthor said. "At last, it will be mine."

"Allow me," the wizard offered.

CRACKLE!

A tendril of magic spun from his fingers and wrapped around the egg. The retrieval spell lifted the object off the stand.

The magical force passed the object through the air and into Luthor's waiting hands.

ZAAAPOWWW!

Luthor disintegrated the egg with his palm blasters.

"What?! Why did you destroy it?" Giganta exclaimed.

"That was just a storage case," Luthor replied with a grin. He held up what looked like a large computer chip for the three villains to see.

Luthor scratched his chin. "Hmm. I will need to make some modifications to interface the Module with my battle suit," he said. "It may take some time, and I'm sure the Big Guy is on his way. Why don't you go out and greet him?"

KA-CRAAASSSH!

The ceiling of the steel chamber collapsed. A figure dressed in blue and red flew down and landed gently in front of them.

"Don't bother. I'm already here," Superman announced.

"Huh, the Big Guy," Solomon Grundy said.

"Why don't you kiddies all play together while I finish this?" Luthor suggested, barely looking up from his task. "It's why I chose you three for this mission."

"How about tag? You're it!" Giganta said as she delivered a powerful punch to Superman.

POWWWW!

The Man of Steel didn't even flinch, but Giganta yelped and rubbed her sore knuckles.

"Who's next?" Superman said.

I'M STRONGER THAN A CHARGING RHINO!
I'M INVULNERABLE, REMEMBER?
OW.
BUT YOU ARE VULNERABLE TO MAGIC!
AHHHHH!
BBOOOOOM!
AHHHHH!

Solomon Grundy, Giganta, and the wizard fell into the crack created by Superman's stomp. They landed in a room below the lab.

"Activate force fields. Voice identity, Superman," ordered the Man of Steel.

Bright beams shot out from the walls of the room. Spheres of light formed around the super-villains. They tried to break free, but the energy globes absorbed their punches. Even The wizard's magic could not penetrate the globe he was trapped inside.

Superman stood at the top of the opening and looked down at the trio. "You can't escape those force fields," he explained. "I tested them against my own powers."

The wizard, Giganta, and Solomon Grundy looked defiant. Then they sat down, defeated.

The wizard grumbled. "I'm not being paid enough for this," he complained.

Giganta gasped. "What? You're getting paid? Luthor is such a cheater!"

"Hmm. Luthor," Superman wondered. "Where is that evil genius?"

"Are you looking for me?" a familiar voice boomed.

"Luthor!" Superman said.

"In the flesh!" Luthor declared. "More accurately, in the battle suit that will destroy you once and for all!"

"You always say that," Superman said.

WOOOOOOSH!

He flew toward Luthor at tremendous speed.

BAAA-BLAAAAAM!

The Man of Steel hit his enemy with super-strength. He grabbed Luthor and his battle suit.

SMASH!

CRASH!

BASH!

Superman smashed upward through the floors and ceilings of a dozen labs. The sound wave blasted past every level of the building.

I have to get Luthor away from all those innocent technicians and workers, Superman thought.

The Man of Steel carried Luthor and the battle suit into the open skies above Metropolis.

KA-ZIRRRRT!

A sudden burst of energy from Luthor's armor caught Superman by surprise and made him release his hold.

There was a second surprise: the burst was painful!

"That was red-sun energy," Luthor said. "I discovered the solar frequency of Krypton's red sun, which is one of the few things that weakens you."

Luthor broke away from Superman's grip.

FWOOOSH!

Flight jets on the battle suit flared as Luthor hovered in the air near the Man of Steel. "I built red-sun defenses into my new, upgraded battle armor," he said. "The Mega Module I took from S.T.A.R. Labs increases the power of my battle suit — along with every other weapon onboard. Let's test it out . . ."

CHAPTER 2

BATTLE FIELD-TEST

Luthor faced Superman, flexing the arms of his armored battle suit. “Let’s see which one of us is the real Man of Steel!” Luthor cried.

Luthor had barely finished his challenge when Superman unleashed a superpowered punch.

THWACK!

Luthor and his suit went soaring high into the sky.

“Armor durability, check,” Luthor observed calmly.

WHAAAAM!

Superman smashed into the battle suit again. This time, Luthor plunged toward the ground.

WHOMP! WHOMP! WHOMP!

Luthor fell through several stories of an abandoned building. He hit the earth with stupendous force, and the building collapsed on top of him.

Superman floated down to where the rubble lay atop Luthor and his battle suit. He hovered above the mound of debris.

"New battle suit, same old ending," said the Man of Steel.

Suddenly the pile of rubble started to shake and fall apart. A shrill sound radiated out from under the collapsed building.

KA-BOOOOSH!

The ruins exploded outward, and Luthor rose into the air.

"Shock absorption systems, check. Sonic wave cannon, check," Luthor said.

"Okay, let's test the heat absorption systems," Superman suggested.

The Man of Steel directed his heat vision at the armor.

ZRRRRRRRRRT!

The blazing blast flared against the red-sun force field surrounding the battle suit. The force field glowed crimson. Inside the suit, Luthor stayed as cool as an ice cube.

"Heat absorption systems, check. Shield integrity, check. Power levels, unlimited," Luthor declared. "The Mega Module is working perfectly."

Superman noticed the shiny computer chip mounted on the chest of the suit.

"So that's what you and your pals were doing at S.T.A.R. Labs. You were after the Mega Module," the Man of Steel said. "It's dangerous, Luthor. The Module is experimental. Unstable."

"It's also powerful, Superman, and it will help me defeat you once and for all!" Luthor boasted.

ZAP!

A sizzling beam of green energy shot out from a fingertip on the glove of the battle suit. The beam hit Superman in the chest. Even though the Man of Steel was invulnerable under the rays of Earth's yellow sun, the green energy burned like fire.

Superman gasped in pain. "Gah!"

"I discovered the frequency for Green Kryptonite, too," Luthor said. "I like to think of it as giving you a little poisoned taste of home."

ZZZTT!
AND THEN THERE'S RED KRYPTONITE!
MY FINGERS CAN FIRE THREE DIFFERENT TYPES OF KRYPTONITE.
THREE DIGITS OF DOOM FOR SUPERMAN!
BOOM!

The furious force of the blast hurled Superman and Luthor in opposite directions. The two combatants tumbled away from each other through the air at tremendous speed. Luthor was shaken inside the metal armor.

"Warning! Shock absorption systems failure," the battle suit announced.

"Uhhh! I'll have to adjust that," Luthor said as his head knocked against the collar of the battle suit.

"Negative control. Negative control," the battle suit's automatic systems informed Luthor.

"I'm taking over manual control. Flight jets, activate," Luthor instructed.

The battle suit obeyed Luthor's commands. The tumbling stopped.

"Locate Superman," Luthor said to the suit.

"Superman located," the suit replied. "Incoming."

The only thing that Luthor saw was a blur of red and blue. Then he was hit with a force as strong as a meteor.

KA-WHAAAM!

Superman slammed into the battle suit before Luthor could even think, let alone voice another command.

Red Kryptonite radiation will make me behave in unpredictable ways, he thought. *I can't let Lex fire it at me again!*

SLAM-BAM-WHAM!

The Man of Steel pounded on Luthor's super armor. He hit it with his fists and heat vision. The red-sun force field around Lex's suit glowed like a red star even though it was daytime.

Luthor fired the flight jets, and the two combatants plunged toward the ground.

SMAAAASH!

They crashed into the docks of Metropolis Harbor, where a warehouse broke their fall.

FWOOOSH!

The heat from the over-worked force field caused the contents of the warehouse to catch on fire. Workers ran away to escape the flames.

"Help! Help!" came a cry from above.

Superman looked up and saw a man trapped in a cargo crane. The blaze burned at the base of the crane. The worker could not climb down, nor jump to safety.

"I have to save that man and fight Luthor at the same time," said the Man of Steel. "I'll have to multi-task."

WHOOOOOSH!

Superman used a gust of his super-breath to blow out the flames like a candle on a birthday cake. Then, without stopping, he turned the breath on Luthor.

KRASHH!!
LEXCORP
HOW DO YOU LIKE MY AIM?
ZAP!
ZAP! ZAP!
YOU WRECKED MY OFFICE! NOW I'M MAD!
ZAP! ZAP!

"Mad?" Superman said as he dodged the energy bolts at super-speed. "You should take some anger management classes. It might help the stress from living a high-profile life as a legitimate businessman."

Furious, Luthor fired the Green Kryptonite energy pulses at random. Superman moved with super-speed. As soon as Luthor shot a blast in one direction, the Man of Steel was somewhere else. By the time Luthor stopped, his fancy office was completely ruined.

"Arrrgh!" Luthor roared. Then he saw something beyond the shattered windows that made him laugh. "Turnabout is fair play, Superman. So let's see how you like it when I destroy something precious to you!"

FWISH!

A small missile launcher popped up from the battle suit. Luthor aimed it at an object behind the Man of Steel.

Superman turned to see what it was just as Luthor fired the missile. "No!" Superman shouted.

FWOOOSH!

The explosive raced toward the *Daily Planet* helicopter hovering just outside the window. While Superman's back was turned, Luthor fired a blast of Green Kryptonite energy at the Man of Steel.

Superman staggered from the force of the strike. Luthor laughed as he watched his foe stumble toward the window. Then Luthor howled with rage as he saw Superman leap from the opening and drop toward the stricken helicopter.

"You won't get away from me," Luthor declared. "I'll get you."

BOOOOOM!

The missile hit the steering rotor, and the pilot lost control.

Lois Lane and Jimmy Olsen grabbed the safety straps in the *Daily Planet* helicopter while the pilot struggled to keep the craft in the air.

"Hang on back there! It's going to be a rough landing," the pilot shouted over the sound of emergency alarms.

Lois pointed to the red-and-blue blur hurtling toward them. "Maybe not as rough as you think. Look — it's Superman!"

"But what's that chasing him?" Jimmy wondered aloud.

CHAPTER 3

BATTLEFIELD METROPOLIS

Superman caught the falling helicopter by its tail section. He used his super-strength to keep the aircraft level as he slowed its descent. Lois Lane leaned out of the open sliding door and watched her friend save them from certain destruction.

"Thanks for the rescue, Superman — again!" Lois said and waved.

"I'm glad to help," said the Man of Steel.

Jimmy snapped some pictures of the Man of Steel. The camera's viewfinder magnified the object coming toward them. "Uh, Superman," Jimmy said, lowering the camera. "Not to interrupt you when you're saving us and all, but what's that behind you?"

"Look out! That thing is firing a laser!" Lois warned.

The thing was Luthor in his battle suit, and the laser was a blast of glimmering red-sun energy.

ZAP!

The brilliant beam hit Superman in the back. Suddenly he felt as if all the strength was draining from his body. He could barely hold the helicopter. His grip weakened and the aircraft slipped.

"No!" Superman cried.

Luthor hovered in the air above the Man of Steel.

ZAP!

ZAP!

ZAP!

Luthor continued to fire the red-sun laser at his enemy. Superman faltered and the helicopter lurched, but the Man of Steel didn't release his grip. He grasped the metal so hard that it dented.

"You're a coward for hitting Superman in the back!" Lois Lane yelled at Luthor.

Lois had plenty more to say, but she was silenced as the helicopter hit the ground.

THHHUUUD!

The impact tumbled the pilot and passengers inside the aircraft. It took a while for Lois's head to stop spinning.

Eventually, Lois was able to check on Jimmy and the pilot. "Are you guys okay?" she asked.

Jimmy gave her a weak thumbs-up. "Good," Lois said. "I need to check on Superman."

Lois climbed out of the overturned helicopter. At first she didn't see the Man of Steel. Then she realized that he was under the aircraft. It had rolled over him, meaning he'd slid underneath it to soften the blow as it crashed into the ground.

Oh, no! Lois thought. *Superman had been blasted with Kryptonite before he caught the falling helicopter . . . Superman could be seriously injured!*

A cold shiver ran down Lois's spine. "Superman!" she cried out and ran toward the fallen hero. But Luthor was faster.

THUD!

VICTORY AT LAST!
I'VE DEFEATED YOU, SUPERMAN...
DAILY PLANET
...AND NOW I WILL DESTROY YOU.
WHOOSH!
NOW I'M THE REAL MAN OF STEEL.

Superman's eyes blinked open. "Clothes do not make the man," he said.

KA-POW!

He delivered a punch that sent Luthor and his battle suit soaring into the air.

"Superman! We thought you were . . ." Lois started to say.

Superman winked. "I was just resting," The Man of Steel assured her. "It takes a lot more than Luthor wearing a fancy tin can to destroy me."

Jimmy shouted and pointed to the skies above. "Look! Something's going on up there!"

BOOOOM!

BOOOM!

The sound of exploding missiles reached their ears. Suddenly a squadron of fighter jets zoomed overhead.

The jets banked sharply and headed toward the bursts. Even without using his super-senses, Superman could hear the sound of weapons firing.

"Duty calls," Superman said and took off with the speed of a supersonic jet.

"Glad you could join the party, Superman," Luthor laughed when Superman arrived. "We're playing pin-the-missile-on-a-jet-fighter. So far, I'm winning."

Superman saw the smoke trails of several falling aircrafts. He did not see any floating parachutes. That meant the pilots were still in the planes!

ZOOOOM!

Superman sped toward them at super-speed.

The Man of Steel grabbed the first plane by one of its wings. With his super-strength, it was like holding onto a toy. The pilot looked shocked when his aircraft stopped falling and started to climb.

"Don't worry, I've got you," Superman told the pilot.

With the plane in one hand, Superman raced to catch the second fighter jet.

SWOOOOOOSH!

Superman arrived just before the aircraft was about to crash into Metropolis Harbor. He used his free hand to grab the tail, then he placed it on top of the first jet like a stack of titanium pancakes.

"One more to go," said the Man of Steel as he sped toward the last jet.

FWUMP!

Superman caught the falling plane before it crashed into a building. There wasn't a pilot in the cockpit. Superman scanned the skies with his super-vision and spotted the white billow of a drifting parachute. The pilot had escaped! Superman exhaled a sigh of relief. Then he used his super-breath to blow the parachute to a safe landing spot.

FWOOOOOOSH!

Suddenly Superman was hit with a barrage of different-colored Kryptonite blasts.

ZAAAT!

ZAAAT!

He stumbled under the onslaught, nearly dropping the aircraft he held, barely avoiding the red Kryptonite blast.

Each one of those Kryptonite blasts is dangerous, Superman thought. *But all three together could destroy me. I have to disable that weapon!*

zZZZRRRRRTT!!
THIS SHOULD RATTLE LUTHOR.
UHHH!

Negative control. Negative human interface.
Autonomous systems engaged.
WHAT AUTONOMOUS SYSTEM? I DIDN'T DESIGN THAT!
Modifications complete. All systems activated.
Mission: destroy Superman!

Suddenly Luthor was trapped inside the battle suit. He had no control over his creation. "The Mega Module must have changed the programming of my battle suit," Luthor realized. "But how did it do that? The Module is supposed to be just a power source!"

Superman's earlier warning rang in Luthor's memory: The Mega Module is experimental. Unstable. Lex hated to admit it, but the Man of Steel had been right.

The robot battle suit now had a mind of its own. It rushed toward Superman as he placed the fighter jets down on a rooftop.

POWWWW!

It slammed into the Man of Steel with tremendous speed. Superman and the battle suit flew off the rooftop and crashed through several nearby buildings.

SMASH! SMASH! SMASH!

The suit's powerful flight jets fired and propelled them toward the ground. They hit with a force that shattered pavement and windows for a block. People were knocked to the ground. Cars were tossed into the air.

Superman and the robot lay in the bottom of the small crater the impact had made. The red-sun force field glowed a dull crimson. Superman's costume smoldered where it touched the force field.

This thing will destroy Metropolis, Superman thought. *I have to get it away from the city. And fast!*

The Man of Steel tucked his hands and feet under the robot and used all four limbs to give it a shove into the air. Superman followed as it flew out of sight.

"Luthor has lost control of his own weapon," observed the Man of Steel. "It looks like I have to rescue him from his own invention."

CHAPTER 4

Superman caught up with the robot battle suit as it tumbled through the air. It did not fire its flight jets to correct or control its course.

"Hm. Maybe the suit was damaged when I hit it with that plane," Superman considered. "I can take advantage of that."

KA-POWWW!

The Man of Steel swooped in and delivered a superpowered punch.

The shot sent the robot hurtling toward the ground. The battle suit plummeted down at the speed of sound.

CRUNCH!

It crashed into the solid stone of a granite quarry.

CRAAAAKK!

CRAAAKKK!

The rock fractured into a spiderweb of fissures around the robot. It did not move. Superman floated down and landed next to the fallen battle robot.

"Are you deactivated, or just resting?" asked the Man of Steel suspiciously. "That was too easy."

Suddenly a thick beam of red energy lanced out from the battle suit.

ZAP!!!

It hit Superman in the middle of his S-shield. The material of his suit started to sizzle.

"Okay, that answers my question. Just resting," the Man of Steel said as he leaped away from the intense heat.

The battle robot got to its feet and fired a wide beam of red-sun energy at the Man of Steel.

KIRSSSSSH!

Superman dodged the onslaught using his super-speed. The blast hit the rock wall of the quarry and shattered it into pebbles.

"You should get a job mining minerals," Superman observed.

"That directive is not within my mission parameters," the robot suit replied. "My only objective is to destroy Superman!"

No sense of humor, Superman thought. *Reminds me of another cranky robot I know.*

RUMMMMMMMBLE!

Suddenly the rock quarry erupted around both Superman and his robot foe. The ground lifted up under their feet and threw them into the air. Pulverized stone swirled around them like snow in a blizzard.

Superman twirled around and around. Finally, he was able to stabilize his flight.

WHIR-WHIR-WHIR-WHIR!

That's when he saw the squad of military combat helicopters above the quarry. A second later they fired another salvo of missiles at the battle robot.

KABOOM!

KABOOOM!

A FEW MILITARY MISSILES WON'T STOP THIS BATTLE SUIT GONE BAD.
LET'S COOL THINGS DOWN!
WHOOOSH!
WHAT?!
CRACKK!

"It looks like the combination of my freeze breath and the force of that missile weakened the suit's force field," Superman said. "If I can disable it, I can stop that rampaging robot!"

Suddenly the battle robot launched into the air. It headed straight for one of the helicopters. Before Superman could stop it, the battle suit grabbed the aircraft by the tail and threw it at the Man of Steel.

"Yaaaa!" the pilots yelled.

"What is it with helicopters today?" Superman wondered as he caught the tumbling machine.

ZRRT-CRACKLE!

Suddenly a wide beam of red-sun energy bathed Superman.

ZRRRRRRRRRT!

The strength drained out of his body. The helicopter became too heavy to hold. The Man of Steel groaned with the effort to keep the aircraft from crashing to the ground.

As the Man of Steel struggled to save the helicopter and its crew, the robot battle suit continued to fire the red-sun energy beam at its target. It was relentless in its goal. It was emotionless at the sight of his faltering enemy. It did not feel triumph.

Trapped inside the battle suit, Luthor wanted to feel victorious but was more concerned about regaining control of his device. He was in danger every second that the armor was independent. Besides, he wanted to be the one to defeat Superman—not some dumb robot! He refused to let a mindless robot succeed while his genius failed.

Luthor could only watch through the internal display monitors as the battle robot pursued Superman. The red-sun energy beam had forced the Man of Steel to his knees. The helicopter weighed down on him as he held it above his head. Slowly the aircraft began to press him into the ground.

ZA-POW! ZA-POW!

Energy blasts bounced off the robot's force field. The helicopter pilots and crew had escaped the helicopter and were firing at the menace that threatened Superman. The shots were not effective against the force field, but they distracted the robot. It automatically turned the red-sun energy beam toward the airmen and away from the Man of Steel.

"Thank you, soldiers," Superman said as his strength returned. He swung the empty helicopter by its landing struts and whacked the battle robot with it.

LET'S FINISH THIS BATTLE ONCE AND FOR ALL.
SUPER-STRENGTH IS BACK...
FWACK!!
SO'S MY HEAT VISION...
FREEZE BREATH TOO!

WHAAAM!

"It's the end of the line for Battle Suit Luthor," Superman said.

He stepped back and admired his handiwork. The metal suit was now encased in ice and solid granite. "Luthor claimed to be the real Man of Steel," Superman said. "But it looks like he turned out to be the real man of rock."

He used an intense beam of heat vision to carve a rough circle into the stone. The line was his guide as he dug into the rock with his invulnerable fingers.

CRUNCH!

CRUMBLE!

Superman hammered out the section of rock that contained the battle robot. He gripped the giant boulder and lifted it over his head.

The General jumped out of his command helicopter.

"You look like Atlas holding the Earth on his shoulders!" the General shouted at Superman.

"Sometimes I think Atlas had it easy," Superman replied with a grin.

The General marched over to the Man of Steel and gave him a sturdy slap on the shoulder to congratulate him. The remaining squads of aircraft landed nearby.

"All strike teams, stand down. The threat has been contained — literally," the General ordered over a headset. "Secure Transport Unit, you may begin your retrieval."

"S.T.U. on the way, sir!" a clear voice responded.

"We'll take care of that thing, Superman. You can put it down now," the General said.

Suddenly a vibration ran down Superman's arms.

The vibration wasn't much at first, but then it started to increase. The boulder shook in his hands.

Something was happening to the rock containing the robot battle suit!

SKREEEEEE!

A shrill sound assaulted their ears. As the sound increased, so did the vibration against the rock in Superman's hands.

"It's coming from inside!" Superman realized.

The General and his airmen crouched for cover and covered their ears. The sonic attack radiated outward from the boulder. The General tried to shout commands above the intense sound. His words could not be heard. His headset shattered.

ZZZRRRTTT!

Suddenly all communication was lost.

CHAPTER 5

CRACK!

The granite boulder holding the robot battle suit shattered. The robot was free! Its flight jets flared as it hovered above the Man of Steel. The high-pitched sound was even louder now. It was coming from raised segments on the battle suit's gloves.

Sonic emitters, Superman realized.

The robot used sound to vibrate the rock until it broke.

Everyone around the Man of Steel was affected by the shrill squeal. The General and his airmen collapsed to the ground, knocked unconscious by the audible attack. Birds dropped from the sky and squirrels fell from the trees. Only Superman remained standing.

"Ugh. I don't like this song," the Man of Steel said. "Let's try a different tune,"

He used his super-hearing to identify the frequency of the sound the robot was projecting. Once he knew that, Superman pitched his voice at a level that sent a wave of sound to counteract the robot's sonic wavelength.

FZZT!

CRACKLE!

The two frequencies canceled each other out.

Realizing that the sonic tactic wasn't working, the battle robot switched attack modes. It fired a small rocket at the Man of Steel.

FACHOOOM!

It struck Superman on his invulnerable chest and disintegrated into a cloud of green dust.

"Kryptonite gas!" Superman moaned as he stumbled backward.

The battle robot pursued the Man of Steel as he staggered toward one of the military helicopters. The robot fired more rockets, forcing Superman back against the metal skin of the aircraft.

Suddenly the onslaught stopped. Superman slumped to the ground. He leaned against one of the landing struts, too weak to stand. He felt as if every muscle in his body was made of overcooked noodles.

The battle robot marched over to the groggy super hero. It stared down at the Man of Steel but made no move to finish him off. Unbeknownst to anyone else, inside his suit, Luthor was fighting to regain control of his creation.

"No! No! Superman is mine to destroy!" Luthor shouted angrily.

The conflicting commands made the battle robot hesitate. As Lex's mind fought for control of the suit, Superman could tell that something was wrong.

Now is my chance to act, Superman thought. *But how?*

Then Superman remembered that the combination of his freeze breath and the explosive force of a military missile had weakened the robot's force field earlier. If he recreated those conditions, he could make the force field fail.

"It's time for a one-two punch to end this fight," Superman said.

ONE...
FWOOOOOSH
SSSSSSS
TWO!
BOOM!

Superman was surrounded by a blizzard of pulverized ice particles. He bent over and put his hands on his knees to brace his body as he recovered from the Kryptonite dust. The blast had shaken the Man of Steel, and that was something he was not used to.

The battle robot lay on its back not far away. The red-sun force field sputtered and sparked. Its vibrant scarlet color had faded to a pale pink. Inside the suit, Luthor worked to regain control. The module had been damaged by the blast. The systems cut in and out.

Luthor knew that he was vulnerable as long as the battle suit was semi-operational. Neither he nor the robot was in control. The armor was defenseless.

"Code LL Omega! Override! Override! Get up, you big tin can!" Luthor yelled.

FZZZZRRRT!

ZRAAATTT!

Sparks erupted inside the helmet. The visual display monitor hissed with static.

But at last the manual control systems lit up. The robot head folded back into the armor. The mutant part of the suit retracted and became inactive.

"I'm back in business," Luthor said triumphantly. "Now where was I before I was so rudely interrupted? Oh, right . . . destroying Superman!"

Lex rose to his feet. Superman heard the heavy thump of armored feet stomp toward him. He was still hunched over from the Kryptonite assault, but he knew what was coming. His eyes flared red as he prepared his heat vision.

"I'm back in the saddle, Superman," Luthor announced.

"More like the hot seat, Luthor!"

ZZZZZRRRRRRRT!

Superman's searing blast of heat vision hit the battle suit in the weakened part of the force field. Superman concentrated his super-vision on the spot and increased the intensity.

SWIRRRRRRSH!

The red-sun energy blazed like a ball of stellar fire.

"Divert energy to the force field," Luthor commanded inside the suit. "It's getting warm in here."

"Heat absorption systems failing," the computer informed Luthor.

"Tell me something I don't know," Luthor grumbled. Sweat rolled down from his forehead.

"Force field failing," the computer responded.

"Not what I meant," Luthor growled.

"Clarify instructions," the computer requested. "Unable to respond. Negative. Negative."

Luthor realized he was losing control of his battle suit. Again! The computer was going haywire. The scientific genius part of him wanted to analyze the problem and design a fix for it. The obsessed man with a grudge against Superman wanted to defeat his enemy at all costs.

The obsessed man won out. "Fire all weapons!" Luthor ordered. This would be his last stand. "Full power to the Kryptonite beams!"

Multiple rays of Kryptonite blasted from the fingers of the battle suit's gloves. A deadly rainbow hurtled toward the Man of Steel. So did the red-sun energy beam and the last of the Kryptonite missiles. Every weapon attacked Superman at the same time!

IT'S YOU OR ME, SUPERMAN!
ZZZTT!
ZZZTT!
ZZZTT!
NOT TODAY, LUTHOR.
NOT...
...EVER!

IS THAT ALL YOU'VE GOT, MAN OF STEEL?
sSSSSSSS
TSSSSSSS
IF YOU WANT TO BE A REAL MAN MADE OF STEEL, THEN HERE'S A LITTLE TASTE.
THUNK!

Superman stood over Luthor's fallen battle suit. The red-sun force field was gone. The Man of Steel reached down and cracked open the armor like it was a thin candy shell. Luthor squirmed inside the battle suit that was now his prison.

"You may have defeated me this time, but it isn't over," Luthor declared.

"You always say that," Superman replied.

"Lex Luthor, you're coming with me!" the General announced.

RUMMMMMMBLE!

The Secure Transport Unit inched to a halt nearby. Its thick metal doors hissed open, ready to receive Luthor.

CRRRREAAAAK!

Superman peeled the battle suit off Luthor.

Superman removed the Mega Module and handed it to the General.

"Please return this to S.T.A.R. Labs," the Man of Steel said. "I'll dispose of the armor myself."

Superman took the battle suit and flew into the sky. He ascended as far as the edge of space. There, he threw Luthor's battle armor on a trajectory toward the sun.

"There's only one Man of Steel," he said as he watched the battle suit disappear into the dark. "The real one."

BIOGRAPHIES

Laurie Sutton has read comics ever since she was a kid. She grew up to become an editor for Marvel, DC Comics, Starblaze, and Tekno Comix. She has written Adam Strange for DC Comics, Star Trek: Voyager for Marvel, plus Star Trek: Deep Space Nine and Witch Hunter for Malibu Comics. There are long boxes of comics in her closet where there should be clothing and shoes. Laurie has lived all over the world, and currently resides in Florida.

Luciano Vecchio was born in 1982 and currently lives in Buenos Aires, Argentina. With experience in illustration, animation, and comics, his works have been published in the US, Spain, the UK, France, and Argentina. His credits include Ben 10 (DC Comics), Cruel Thing (Norma), Unseen Tribe (Zuda Comics), and Sentinels (Drumfish Productions).

SKETCHES

FINAL ART

WHOOSH!
CRACKK!

ZZZTT!
ZZZTT!
ZZZTT!
MASH!!
CRASHHH!!
ZZZTT!
ZZZTT!
ZZZTT!
ZZZTT!
ZZZTT!
ZZZTT!
ZZZTT!

caption (KAP-shuhn)—words that appear in a box. Captions are often used to set the scene.

gutter (GUHT-er)—the space between panels or pages

motion lines (MOH-shuhn LINES)—illustrator-created marks that help show motion in art

panel (PAN-uhl)—a single drawing that has borders around it. Each panel is a separate scene on a spread.

SFX (ESS-EFF-EKS)—short for sound effects. Sound effects are words used to show sounds that occur in the art of a comic.

splash (SPLASH)—a large illustration that often covers a full page (or more)

spread (SPRED)—two side-by-side pages in a comic book

word balloon (WURD BUH-loon)—a speech indicator that includes a character's dialogue or thoughts. A word balloon's tail leads to the speaking character's mouth.

GLOSSARY

conjure (KON-jer)—to make something appear or seem to appear by using magic

crude (CROOD)—very simple or basic, or done in a way that does not show a lot of skill

disintegrated (diss-IN-tuh-gray-tid)—to break apart into many small parts or tiny pieces

frequency (FREE-kwen-see)—the number of times that something (such as a sound wave) is repeated in a period of time

hesitate (HEZ-uh-tate)—to stop briefly before you do something

invulnerable (in-VUHL-ner-uh-buhl)—unable to be harmed or damaged

modifications (mod-if-uh-KAY-shuhn)—changes made to the parts of something

onslaught (ON-slot)—a violent attack

technicians (tek-NISH-uhnz)—people whose job relates to the practical use of machines or science in industry, medicine, etc.

VISUAL QUESTIONS

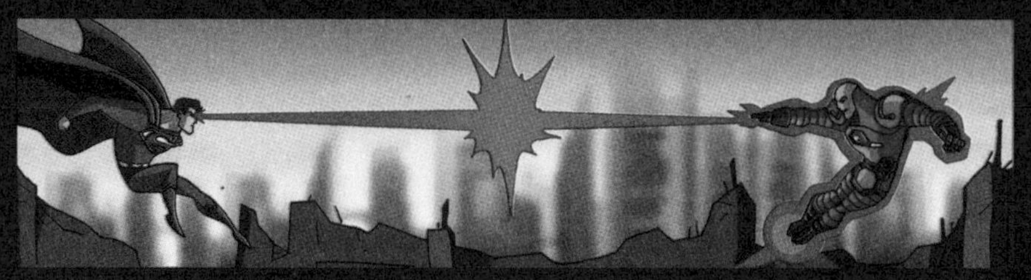

1. Lex Luthor battles Superman with his battle suit. Which would you rather have: Superman's superpowers or Lex's suit? Why?

2. In their battle, Lex occasionally gets the upper hand on Superman, but the Man of Steel always finds a way to win. What tricks did Superman use to get the better of Lex? Find as many as you can.

3. Superman uses his heat vision to melt metal on Lex's hands. How do you think Lex managed to get his hands free? Would you help free Lex?

4. When Lex's battle suit takes over, Lex loses control of his suit. What caused this to happen? Whose fault is it?

5. The armed forces attempt to help Superman defeat Lex, but they don't help all that much. What are some ways they could've supported the Man of Steel?